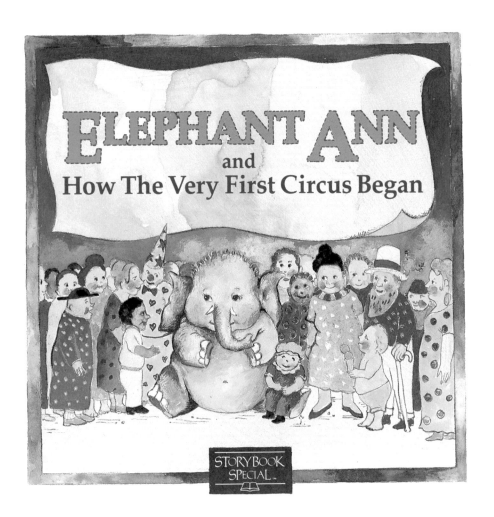

ELEPHANT ANN
and
How The Very First Circus Began

STORYBOOK SPECIAL™

by

Jon Madian

illustrated by

Kathy Jacobi

PRICE STERN SLOAN
Los Angeles

To my mother Ann and my daughter Andrea
J.M.

For my darling Richard and Arie
K.J.

©1988 by Jon Madian and Kathy Jacobi

Published by Price Stern Sloan, Inc.
360 North La Cienega Boulevard,
Los Angeles, California 90048

ISBN: 0-8431-2260-9

Have you ever wondered which came first, the elephant, the circus or the tent? Well, this is the story of Elephant Ann and how the *very first* circus began. Once upon a time there were no circuses and no circus tents.

Of course there were
lions and tigers. And there were jugglers
and clowns in the towns. And there were
elephants to be found everywhere, but
absolutely no circuses.

Perhaps there never would
have been a circus had Elephant Ann, a small and
sweet elephant, not sneezed . . .

then coughed . . .

and finally blown, and blown and blown her
poor, long, runny nose.

On that night the villagers
woke again and again while their little houses shook
and shook from Elephant Ann's coughs. In the morning,
when the people saw how miserable poor Ann was,
sneezing and wheezing, coughing and blowing . . .

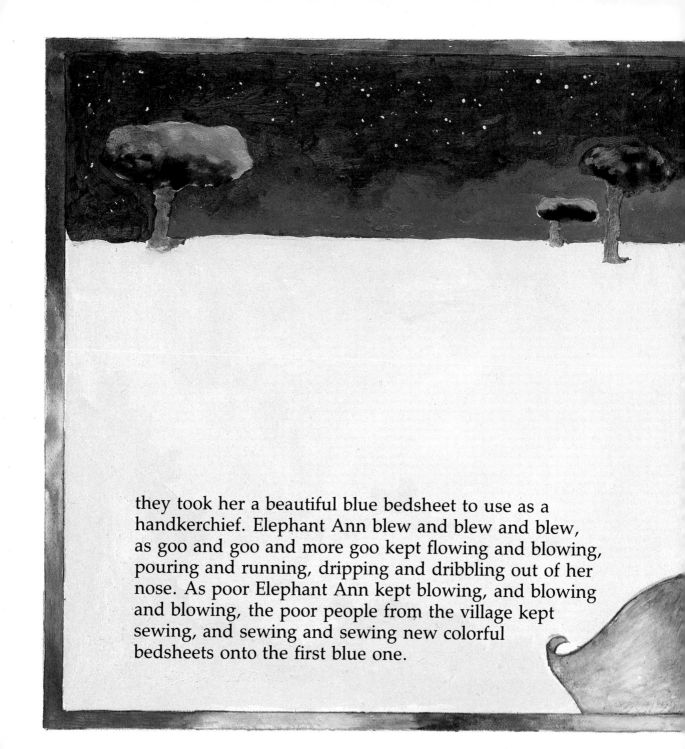

they took her a beautiful blue bedsheet to use as a
handkerchief. Elephant Ann blew and blew and blew,
as goo and goo and more goo kept flowing and blowing,
pouring and running, dripping and dribbling out of her
nose. As poor Elephant Ann kept blowing, and blowing
and blowing, the poor people from the village kept
sewing, and sewing and sewing new colorful
bedsheets onto the first blue one.

They added sheets and more sheets—yellow, green, red and purple, pink and beige and brown. In the midst of all these handkerchiefs sat Elephant Ann, blowing and wiping, sneezing and coughing, dripping and dabbing, and waiting—until finally her nose stopped running.

The people cheered to see
Elephant Ann sitting quietly in the sun resting. They took
the rainbow patchwork of sheets down to the river for a good
washing. They scrubbed and rubbed, rubbed and scrubbed
the colorful bedsheets in the clear cool river. Then they hung
them in the sunny meadow to dry.

As the bright wind blew under the sheets, the sheets billowed and ballooned into the blue sky, billowed like a rainbow of colorful pillows.

A clown from the town
happened down by the meadow. When he saw Elephant Ann
sitting in the sun quietly admiring the beautiful rainbow
colored tent, he skipped underneath. He looked up and
around and laughed and tumbled and did the most
wonderful clown tricks he had ever done.

Wild lions and tigers
wandered from the dark wild woods under the light
bright tent. The lions and tigers did tricks with the
clown, who pretended to be a wild animal trainer.

Jugglers and other clowns came from the town. They juggled and tumbled and somersaulted. The people from the village came and sat by Ann. They laughed at the clowns, clapped for the jugglers and were amazed by the lions and tigers, who jumped through hoops of fire. Next, beautiful men, women and children hung ropes from the tops of the tallest trees. They walked on the ropes high up against the colorful tent top. They swung through the air . . .

and then they let go and did flips
and somersaults and cartwheels,

and then caught each other in mid-air.

Then the elephants came and played.

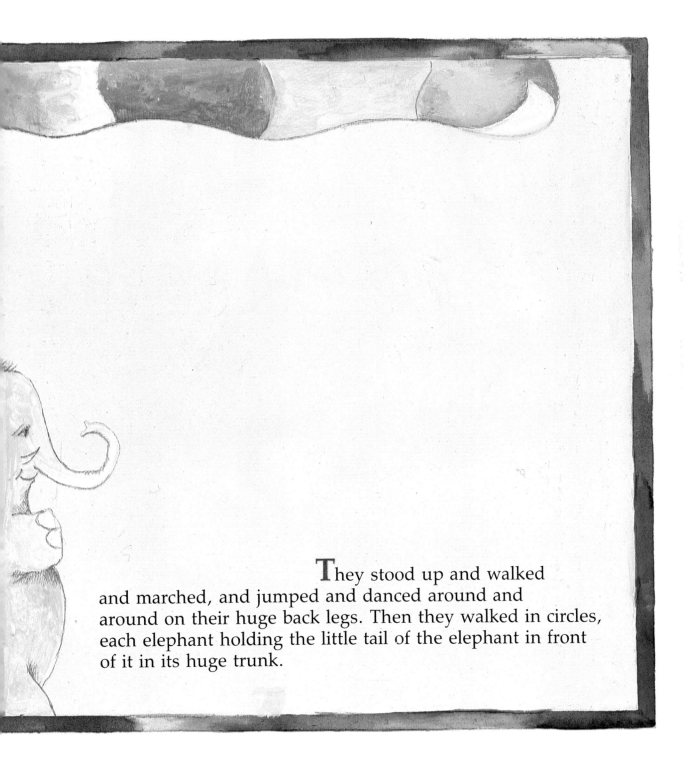

They stood up and walked
and marched, and jumped and danced around and
around on their huge back legs. Then they walked in circles,
each elephant holding the little tail of the elephant in front
of it in its huge trunk.

Finally, the elephants invited everyone for a ride. They lifted babies and young children,

grandmothers and grandfathers,

mothers and fathers, up in their long, strong, round
trunks and placed them on their wide gray backs.

Then, side by side,
everyone had an elephant ride.

Now, from that day to this, whenever an elephant has a cold, afterwards, a circus comes to town and puts up a wonderful tent. Then people go to see the clowns, tigers and lions, jugglers and acrobats. And everyone hopes to ride on an elephant. Then they remember Elephant Ann and how the very first circus began.